MYSTERY THIEF!

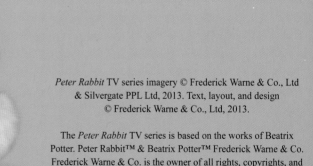

Peter Rabbit TV series imagery © Frederick Warne & Co., Ltd
& Silvergate PPL Ltd, 2013. Text, layout, and design
© Frederick Warne & Co., Ltd, 2013.

The *Peter Rabbit* TV series is based on the works of Beatrix
Potter. Peter Rabbit™ & Beatrix Potter™ Frederick Warne & Co.
Frederick Warne & Co. is the owner of all rights, copyrights, and
trademarks in the Beatrix Potter character names and illustrations.

Published by the Penguin Group. Penguin Group (USA) Inc.,
375 Hudson Street, New York, New York 10014, USA.
Manufactured in China

978-0-7232-8041-5   10 9 8 7 6 5 4 3 2 1

Map of My Woods

This is a map of the woods where I live. You can see who else lives here, too. The map is in my dad's journal, which I always have with me.

ROCKY ISLAND

Cotton-tail is my littlest sister, and the naughtiest!

OLD BROWN'S ISLAND

MR. JEREMY FISHER POND

SQUIRREL NUTKIN'S WOOD

MRS. TIGGY-WINKLE'S LAUNDRY

Squirrel Nutkin has some of the best, and nuttiest, ideas.

Mrs. Tiggy-winkle runs the laundry. She keeps us neat and tidy.

This is **Mr. Tod.** Foxes eat rabbits. Need I say more?

JEMIMA PUDDLE-DUCK'S HILLTOP FARM

MR. MCGREGOR'S GARDEN

MR. TOD & TOMMY BROCK'S WOOD

MY BURROW

DR. & MRS. BOBTAIL'S BURROW

TUNNEL NETWORK

MR. BOUNCER'S BURROW (BENJAMIN'S HOME)

RAVINE

DEEP DARK WOODS

DANDELION FIELD

My friend, **Lily Bobtail.** Whatever the problem, she's got the answer.

My mom— **Mrs. Rabbit** to you! I try to stay on her good side.

Benjamin Bunny is my cousin. Whatever I do, he's right behind me—usually hiding!

One sunny morning, Peter and Benjamin hopped stealthily through Mr. McGregor's vegetable garden scooping up radishes.

Suddenly, Peter Rabbit stopped
in his tracks, twitched his nose,
and pricked up his ears.
"I can hear Mr. McGregor,"
he whispered.

"Let's hop to it!"

Peter tore off through the vegetable garden, with Benjamin close behind. Their mouths were full of stolen radishes, and Mr. McGregor was hot on their heels, shouting . . .

"STOP, thieves!"

Just in time, the bunnies spotted a
secret escape tunnel dug many years
before by Peter's dad for JUST this kind
of emergency. They dived inside.

"Phew!" puffed Peter as they shot out of the other end,
closely followed by 1 ... 2 ... 3 ... 4 juicy radishes.

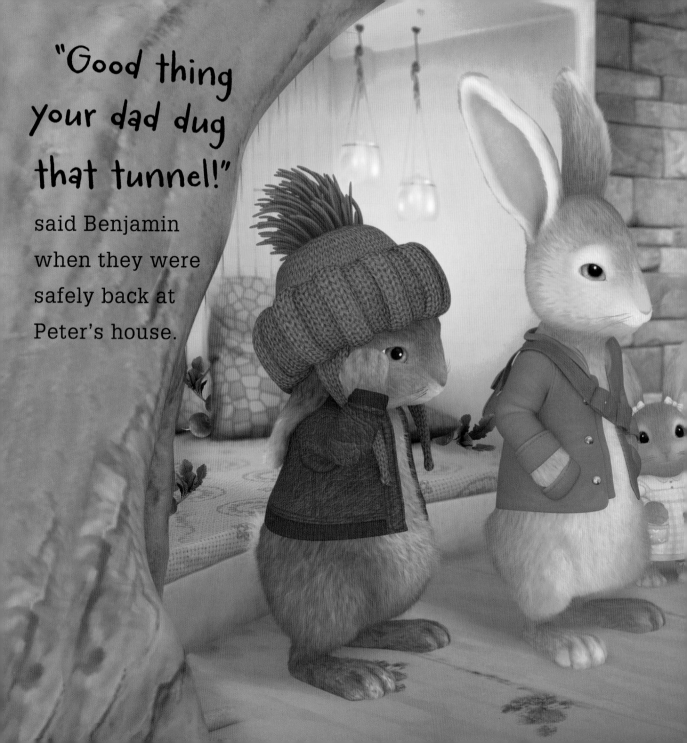

"Good thing your dad dug that tunnel!" said Benjamin when they were safely back at Peter's house.

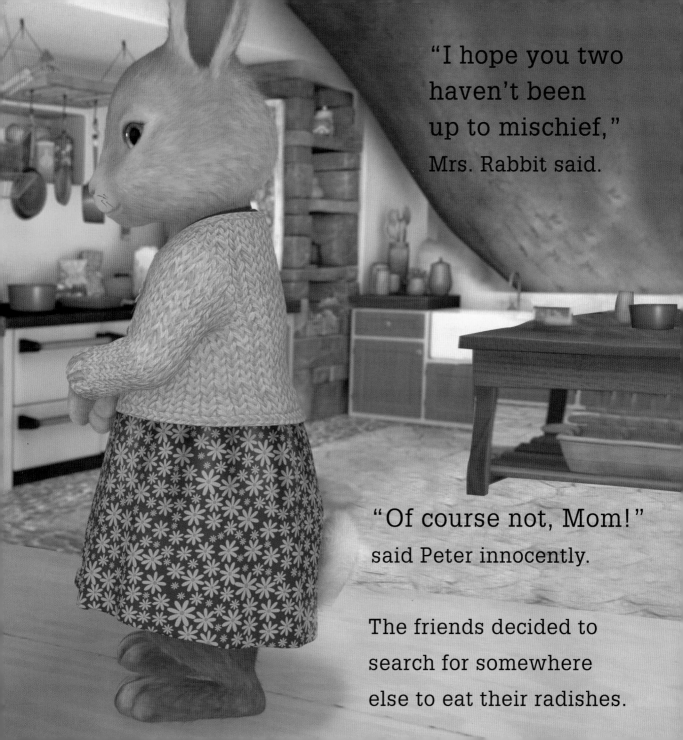

"I hope you two haven't been up to mischief," Mrs. Rabbit said.

"Of course not, Mom!" said Peter innocently.

The friends decided to search for somewhere else to eat their radishes.

Rushing along the path, they met Lily Bobtail on her way to Mrs. Tiggy-winkle's laundry. "Look what we've got, Lily," whispered Peter.

"RADISHES!"

gasped Lily.

"We need somewhere secret to eat them," added Benjamin. "I know just the place," she said, tucking them safely in with the washing. "Come with me."

Mrs. Tiggy-winkle's laundry, high up in the hills, was the perfect secret place to eat the radishes.

"Let's get munching!" said Benjamin, rubbing his tummy.

Peter sniffed around for the secret radish stash.

"Oh no, all the baskets look the same

After some secretive searching, three radishes
were found, BUT . . . there was **ONE** missing.

"Do you think we DROPPED it?"
asked Peter. "Or do you think
someone TOOK it?"

The three hungry rabbits retraced their steps,
in case the radish had dropped out on the path.
"There's no sign of it," said Lily.

"It must have been taken
by a mystery thief."

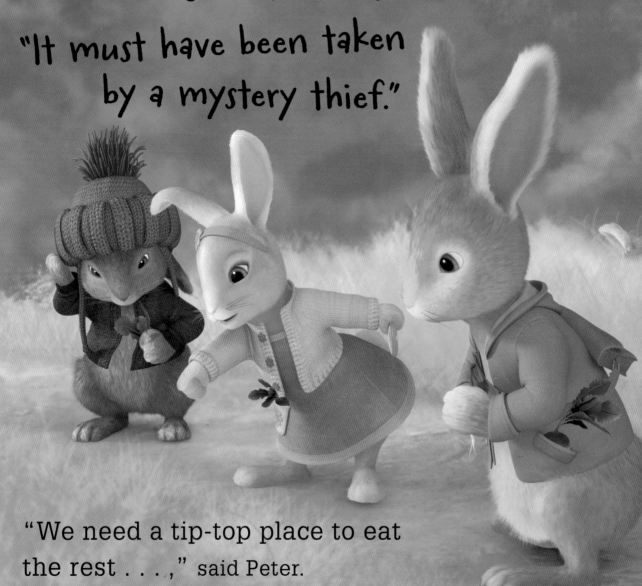

"We need a tip-top place to eat
the rest . . . ," said Peter.

"And it doesn't get much tip-toppier than way up in the Squirrel Camp!"

"Rabbits are brave, rabbits are brave!"

Benjamin whispered to himself.

"Flippety floppety flee!
Three rabbits in a tree!"

sang silly Squirrel Nutkin when
the rabbits arrived at the top.

Reaching down, he snatched
the radishes and started
JUGGLING with them!

"Hey, Nutkin!" called Peter desperately. "Careful with those!" But it was too late, and the precious radishes went whizzing past him . . .

. . . toward the ground.

"A good rabbit never gives up!"

called Peter, swinging down after the radishes as fast as he could.

Lily and Benjamin were more cautious and followed close behind in the elevator.

The radishes landed in the grass
a hop and a jump away from Lily
and Benjamin, but by the time
they'd scampered to find them . . .
there was only **ONE** left.

Had the mystery thief
TAKEN the other **TWO?**

Just as they had decided to split the remaining radish, Peter felt his fur tingle, and spun around. There stood Mr. Tod, **LICKING HIS LIPS.**

As the wily fox came closer, Peter spied an unusual rock.

A rock he'd seen drawn in his dad's journal . . .

"QUICK, EVERYONE! Jump on that rock," said Peter. As the rock lifted off the ground, Peter tossed the radish at Mr. Tod, shouting, "You can have our last radish, but you can't have us!"

"This was what Dad used to outfox that fox!"
laughed Peter as the magical rock shot away and
surfed across the grass.

"Good old Dad!"

Back at the burrow, Cotton-tail
was waiting to greet the tired
and hungry bunnies.

"Hello, Cotton-tail.
What have you been
up to today?"
began Peter.

"And what's that delicious smell?"

added Benjamin, cheering up a little.

"It smells like . . . No, it can't be."

"Radish soup!"
cried Peter.

"Yes." Mrs. Rabbit smiled. "Clever Cotton-tail found all these radishes."

Peter, Benjamin, and Lily gasped . . . and then laughed. "Well done, Cotton-tail," giggled Peter. "Good scavenging!"

Did you guess the **MYSTERY THIEF?**

OUR SECRET BURROWS

Rabbits like us have to hide in a hurry A LOT. These old escape tunnels my dad built are perfect for a quick getaway.

Entrance (hidden under flowerpot)

ONE rabbit at a time

Secret radish stas

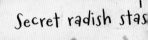

Can You SPOT While You Trot?

There are so many things to spot when you are out and about. Help us find useful things, pretty things, and even tasty things. (Tasty for a rabbit, that is!)

Florence is a ladybug. I know that for a fact!

Cotton-tail spotted lots of radishes.

SEE IF YOU CAN SPOT:

- Three different-shaped leaves
- A pretty flower or two
- A bird, a butterfly, and a bug

CONGRATULATIONS!

SKILL IN SPOTTING CERTIFICATE

Awarded to

_____

_____

Age

_____

Lily Bobtail

LILY BOBTAIL
BEST SPOTTER IN THE WOOD

Super spotting skills!